Memoirs

of a Bad Bitch

Acknowledgements

Thank God that I was born with this awesome talent. Prior to writing this book, I had not written anything for years. I'd just read and critiqued other people's work, but always had the thought in the back of my head that someday, someone would critique my own book.

I've written short stories and mini novels and emailed them to myself, only to re-read them whenever I accessed my emails. I had refrained from calling myself a writer years ago, because everyone knows "real writers cannot stay away from the pen". With that being said, I want to send a huge shout-out to my friend Jarome Gordon. He'd never read my material but the minute I told him I was a writer, he encouraged me to go for it; to write and get published. He made it seem so simple. If he believed in me I had no other option but to believe in myself, right?

Thanks to all my friends and family who believed in me and encouraged me along the way. Shout out to my friends and fans who posted and reposted excerpts from my novel as well as the link to purchase my book. Y'all the real MVPs!

I appreciate all of you. Y'all kept me disciplined and grounded. Y'all practically forced me to finish this book, just to see what happened next with my crazy characters. Thanks guys, it really motivated me.

Lastly, big ups to my little princess who was being a good girl the entire two months it took me to finish this book. Big ups to my Mommy; I love you endlessly even if I don't say it every day. I Know I'm hard to deal with but thanks for your unconditional love and prayers. Continue praying. Whatever prayer you prayed worked. All your kids have their very own talent.

Chapter 1 :
Chyn

I'm far from a dumb bitch. I'm filthy rich and have garnered respect on the streets of Jamaica with my natural "boss lady" aura. People look at me and know that I'm *that* bitch. They perceive that I've got some money, but are clueless about where it comes from. Just the way I like it; low-key with the mullah.

My name is Chyn Dinero. I'm thirty-two years old and am the baddest bitch alive. I was born and raised in the slum of Twelve Lane, a White Hall community. What didn't kill me though, made me stronger and I am the definition of strength and perseverance.

I had my money counter on my coffee table and cash all around me as I sat on my sofa in my snake-skin lingerie with my chin resting on one hand. I peered down on my shiny, red, super-long, blinged-out stiletto nails on the other hand and took a trip down memory lane…

I remember all my friends wanting to attend the community college in our area because we were cheerleaders, and where else would we cheer? I loved cheerleading and wanted to cheer too but that could be done in my spare time.

My dream was to count money for a living. Yea, I wanted to be an accountant, but I also wanted to meet a rich unsuspecting fool who would worship the ground I walked on and make me his wife. I was tired of living in my poverty-stricken Kingston 8 community; I needed a breakthrough. I wanted to live large.

I got registered in college with the last one thousand dollar note that I had. I didn't tell my friends I was dead broke, or that I didn't know how I would pay my tuition. As luck would have it, I got a summer job at a prominent high school.

While working there, the guidance counsellor at the school took a liking to me. His name is Mr.

Knacker. He showed me the ropes and ensured that I was settling in fine. He didn't leave any room for any of the younger men to even try courting me.

I found out through talking to him regularly that he owned and operated a private school as a side hustle. From the day he told me about the private school, he relentlessly tried to convince me to make a visit there. Once I agreed to visit, that's when I learned that the school doubled as a church and that he was also a pastor.

While he taught his Math class, I would lounge in his office. After classes, we spent hours discussing a wide range of topics and ultimately ended the day with him slurping my pussy juices.

Don't judge me, I didn't know he was a pastor until that day.

But…I blackmailed him for money for my first-semester tuition and miscellaneous fees. The idiot had a wife and children, and could not risk getting caught.

The same day I received the monies for fees

and went to the bank to pay it over to the school's account, I bumped into Velasquez. From that day onward, I was a paid bitch.

I was young and sexy. He needed me for a job and a *job*. He thinks that pretty bitches hang with other pretty bitches, so I must've had friends who are young and just as pretty as I am, and I did. He explained to me that all I needed was Google Maps, a great internet connection, transportation and some pretty ladies like myself. The job was to travel all over the island distributing anything from illegal drugs to guns and money. At first, I was doubtful. I was sixteen years old, fresh out of high school, newly enrolled in community college and scared shitless. What if I get caught?

Getting caught invaded my thoughts on many nights before my first job. But on the contrary, getting caught could never be enough of an hindrance for me to not go chasing the bag.

The first time I made "the run", I had an adrenaline rush like no other. We rented a minibus and all of us dressed in our varsity cheerleading uniforms. We were a set of pretty skinny bitches, dressed in uniforms that showed off our midriffs and miniskirts.

We had a minibus with a tank full of gas and a trunk full of guns and ammunition. The minibus was made into a replica of our school bus, so the cops wouldn't bother us. And it worked well because we were able to drive pass the highway police with no problem.

We had enough weapons to aid in a world war, and were fearless and money-hungry. However, for the entire drive to Montego Bay, we were on edge.

It was supposed to be pretty simple. We'd drop off the weapons, collect the cash and drive back to Kingston.

We drove carefully and in absolute silence all the way to Montego Bay, did the drop then drove back to Kingston. The drop was uneventful and I was five hundred thousand dollars richer afterwards. I split the cash evenly as we had all taken the same risk. At the end of the drop, I became known to my friends as the "hook up" to make some quick cash.

Call me the unofficial plug.

But I don't do drops anymore. I plan them. When I retrieve the cash from the drops, I count it myself and distribute it at the agreed-upon percentage. The job I do is risky and the money I make may attract traitors, so nobody knows where I really live except Velasquez. Not even my closest friends.

The arms of flesh may fail you, dare not trust your own.

With all the money that I've acquired, I've become very paranoid. But I never want to learn which of my bitches have the nerve to be a snitch or worse, try to take my life or my spot as queen of the streets because….

Snitches get stitches… No cap!

Velasquez has always had his eyes on me. I fucked with him a few times too. However, when he saw how hungry I was, he fed the beast in me. I was no longer his bottom bitch, he turned me into a boss bitch and I'm forever grateful. So whenever he calls, I answer and if he ever needs me, I'm there. No questions asked…. guns blazing!!!

I live my life though, separate and apart from my street persona.

CHAPTER 2:
Chyn

It's hard to find a husband when you're rich, and when you're black. I'd given up the notion by age twenty-five. I was no longer interested in being Cinderella. I don't want to be rescued; I prefer to be the one doing the rescuing. It has always been fuck men and get money. It's not even a case where I've had any awful experiences with guys myself. But if I will be in a relationship, it has to be on my own terms.

I've always been a dominant person, but once I got with Velasquez, things grew worse. He is the plug but is likewise well-known for his notoriety in the streets of Jamaica and in the corporate sector as an investor, internet and aerospace entrepreneur and media proprietor. As rich as he is, nobody has ever associated his name with any female except me. He is also the definition of confidential. He just makes cash and stays to himself.

His hobbies included spoiling me and making money. That's the only thing he did.

He is also three times my age and experienced in everything. Velasquez dropped jewels about life and I paid attention. I stored the knowledge in the back of my head because I felt like someday I'd be using it. He took me on romantic dates, splurged on me and showed me how to be a genuine boss lady.

I watched and mastered all his businesses inside out. I learned to do everything from planting marijuana to reaping it and could cook cocaine, bag it up, distribute it and count the money.

I knew how he laundered his dirty cash, and about all his offshore accounts. I observed how he did private investigations and how to blend into a crowd of people.

I did all of that whilst still attending college and doing my nightly drop-offs. I became his right hand and certified protégé.

I was his queen. I only needed a wedding ring to make it official, and I'd have gotten it too if that was what I wanted.

Velasquez was an impressive man all around. He provided everything I needed, except he couldn't fuck me silly. My friends went on and on about their sex lives and even though I'm the type to listen and never share my personal stories, I couldn't help but think about how my sex life paled in comparison to theirs.

Vel was too elderly and feeble, and too prim and proper.

He had lots of ancient beliefs that I didn't care about.

Our sex life was non-existent because he has an erectile dysfunction. Sweet as he is, he can only eat the pussy and sometimes a girl needed to scratch the itch.

We've had many arguments because he's content with not being able to have traditional sex. He was content with his inefficiency; he felt like once I was having orgasms, that's all that mattered. After too many spats about the very same issue, we decided to part ways.

Don't get it wrong though, I am and will always be queen of the castle. We just weren't on the same wavelength. He thinks the main issue is that I needed to live a little. So, he set me up in a home of my own and promised to give me whatever I desired. He was surprised when all I wanted was to run the city and make my money.

The day I moved into my own house, I exhaled. I didn't even notice I was holding my breath until then. I was relieved to be from up under Velasquez. I was so relieved that I partied hard and spent cash that I hadn't yet earned. I spiralled out of control before I reined myself in and focused on the bigger picture. By then, I was indebted and wasn't about to make Vel know.

I started trying to make extra money while still being flashy and obnoxious. Men flocked me everywhere I went and apart from selling drugs and distributing guns, I searched for a new and younger Vel.

I never met him, though. I encountered men who'd only finance me if they were fucking me, some that I could walk all over, and some that made me vomit just by looking at them. However, I preferred wealthy men that would boss up on me like a motherfucker.

I was never attracted to guys who truly wanted me. I was attracted to the guys that acted nonchalant because I enjoyed the thrill of the chase. If they didn't like me back, I didn't care because ultimately I always get what I want.

Most times after getting what I want though, I no longer wanted it. The mystery disappeared and the prize loses its charm.

Chapter 3:
Kloud

Kloud and his friends sat on the wooden benches that lined the makeshift football field.

All the hoods in east-side Jamaica had a makeshift field that little boys and men frequented, all with the hopes of being the next great footballer.

Kloud sat with a white towel around his neck and his body soaked in his own sweat. The sweat dripped down his body as he was partially clothed in just football shorts and boots. His skin glistened in the sun as he removed his water bottle from his mouth.

"So I met a baddie, and mannnnn she's thicker than a snicker and drives a 2020 Jeep Wrangler", he laughed.

"You have *allll* the luck. Where do you find all these bitches, man?" asked Jerry.

"If you're asking where I met Chyn, I didn't meet her. She met me. Shorty saw me walking out of the gym while she was driving past. She held up traffic while honking her car horn continuously to get my attention. I was in disbelief, so I tried to walk pass like I didn't notice her but she hopped out of her Jeep and approached me. She earned my number. She's a motherfucking savage, yo."

Kloud finished off his water and walked to his car. He sat in his car and thought back to the first time he saw Chyn. She walked like a goddess, hips swaying from side to side hypnotizing him. She was doing a sexy run-walk thing trying to catch up to him.

Her hair had a smooth texture, while it bounced against her buttocks. Not a strand out of place. He had trouble figuring out whether it was her natural tresses or she was wearing a weave.

He shook off the memory of the day he met

Chyn and told his friends goodbye. He then started his car, with thoughts of blowing Chyn's back out.

Shorty bad, no lie. Bad as she is, there isn't a bitch alive bad enough to break up my marriage. None. Period. Fuck em', block em and go home to wifey. That was my mantra.

I'm a dog ass nigga. I like keeping my dick wet and my pockets lined, that's why I keep myself up. I go to the gym. I eat well, sleep well and don't smoke or drink plus I do my regular check-ups.

Most importantly, I don't think about these bitches! I've figured from a very young age that the more you show these women love is the more ruthless they'll treat you. Women are simple creatures that are easily manipulated. They are suckers for bad boys who they think they can reform or rescue.

He turned the key in the ignition, starting his car and turning up the stereo. Lil Wayne's "Love Me" blasted instantly.

Kloud weaved his way through traffic and was home in thirty minutes. He grabbed his phone and

Whatsapp'd Chyn.

"*Fat pussy, Chyn. When will I get the chance to feel my dick going in and out of your fat pussy?*"

She replied, "*Lol.*"

"*Lemme see your tits!*"

"*Not right now, I have company.*"

"*Just a glimpse?*"

She gave in and sent him a picture.

Her breasts were perky and the nipples erected. He gaped at the photo over and over. *Small perfect breasts*, he thought, *with just the cutest heart-shaped nipple rings.*

His mouth watered from the vision on his phone screen and his impure thoughts. His cock rose. *Fuck!!!*

"*Can I swing by to fuck you later?*" He got to the point.

No reply.

He sent another message. "*Please?!!!!*"

Blue ticks. No reply.

Two Hours Later…

Still no reply.

He sent her a video.

* * *

At Chyn's House

She opened the video.

The first thing she saw was his cock and it looked glorious. She eased back in her sofa and watched the video of him pleasuring himself.

Up and down he pumped his penis. It was wet from his pre-cum. Even more sexy was his facial expression.

She was in awe. Stuck in the moment. Lost in the video.

He moved his fingers back and forth on his cock. Over and over, mesmerizing her further and further. He moaned and groaned in the video and she got further carried away.

She was dripping wet and uncomfortable. She had an orgasm just from watching Kloud masturbate.

She decided to reply, *"Come lemme suck the skin off your dick, pappy."*

She threw her phone on the table and proceeded to climb the stairs. She rampaged her chest-of-drawers. She was out of Duracell.

The cat and mouse game was about to end.

The flirting would end today. Kloud was getting fucked.

She picked up her home phone and dialed *Eden's All Women*. She made an appointed to get waxed.

It's better to have a bald pussy than eyebrows on fleek.

Chapter 4:
Chyn

All men are dogs, but Virgo men are the worst set of dogs.

I paced back and forth because I was nervous as fuck. God, please don't let him leave me hanging tonight. Not tonight!

After getting pampered, I messaged Kloud and confirmed plans to meet up. I had treated myself to a day of being pampered, inclusive of a manicure, pedicure, facial, massage, and a perfect wax job. Every part of my body was silky smooth and my vagina was waxed into 'The Hollywood'.

Today is one of my days that I've dedicated to self-care. I'm dead tired, and I should be sleeping but instead, I wanted to feel his big black dick tearing up my insides. Yes! I already had it all planned out. Today is supposed to be "fuck me like a hoe" day. I wanna get fucked, go home, shower and go sleep.

Oh, and ignore his calls and text messages until I felt like fucking again.

It's an unhealthy cycle between myself and my favorite fuck-buddy, Kloud. Yes, that's his real name and it's befitting too because daddy always takes me to Cloud 9.

My day wasn't going as planned and I wasn't about to call him twice. I refuse to call any man on the face of the earth twice in the same day if he doesn't answer the first time.

It was now after 10 pm and my insomnia was at its worst. Sleep evaded me at all costs. Instead, I twisted and turned all over my bed, fluffed the pillows and straightened the sheets. Nothing worked.

I resorted to stooping on the bed. I stared at the black ceiling, played with my hair and even tried to count sheep. Frustrated, I jumped out of bed and paced the room. Sleep still wouldn't come.

So, I got dressed in a hot pink tank top and some black spanks, donned a black Champion running shoes and sprinkled my skin with some Rihanna body mist. I then connected my air buds to my iPhone. After ensuring I attached them, I turned on an old Tanya Stephens *Rebelution* album. I tightened my holster around my leg and was ready to go. I went for a jog.

It was an interminable stretch that was supposed to make me exhausted enough to sleep. It didn't help. I wasn't sleepy. I was more energized after the run than before. My imagination was running wild, and it annoyed me.

I was irritated and fuckstrated.

I couldn't ignore or run from my thoughts of him. I remembered the tattoos on his arms. I wanted to kiss his chest. I enjoyed licking his nipples and observing the goosebumps surface all over his body.

Fuck! I wanted to fuck.

I wanted to fuck him so badly, or I would drive

myself fucking crazy with thoughts of doing so.

I'd remained awake on many nights, with thoughts of Kloud. After a mile-long run and a cold shower, I'd finally reached the realization that I was never going to fall asleep without an orgasm.

I withdrew the blankets from my body and looked up in the mirror that spanned the entire ceiling area of my room, then I looked across from where I laid and marvelled at the golden poles that were also installed on either side of my bed. I'd experienced many a rendezvous in this very room but none of them haunted me like the one I never had.

My body was perfect. I was laying down and my breasts were looking up. The crystals from my nipple rings sparkled in the mirror above me as I admired myself. My belly was non-existent. It was flat as a washboard.

And what waist? I swore I had one of the tiniest waists in the world and my skin was smooth from years of using Shea butter.

I inched down towards the bottom of the bed and opened my legs. I was positioned in a split, one foot planted on each pole.

I closed my eyes even though I knew closing my eyes defeated the purpose of the mirror above me. I desperately needed these hands of mine to be Kloud's.

I imagined he was kissing my neck. I twisted my neck from side to side while palming my breasts with both hands then gently squeezing. My nipples stood erect, and I opened my eyes. When I opened them, there he was standing in my door-way in all his naked masculine glory.

He looked like an angel glistening in the dark, there to rescue me from my darkest sexual abyss.

He walked towards the bed. No words were spoken.

My pussy was creaming and screaming Kloud's name.

Pleaseeee meeee.......

When I opened my eyes, he was on top of me

with his back towards the mirrored ceiling. He was naked with tattoos all over on his broad, muscular back. His thighs looked strong. His ass... looked heavenly! He flicked his tongue on my ultra sensitive nipples and I felt my pussy throb. He kissed my belly button. He then positioned to give me the dick.

The dick.

The dick I was dying to feel. The dick I was dying to taste. The dick I was dying to own.

I don't know exactly how long and how wide it was but he was tearing me up. He did combination strokes. Slow and fast, then fast and slow with one, two, three counts at a steady pace.

He hammered my vagina without mercy. I tried to tell him to stop, but my voice got caught in my throat. My feet trembled and fell from the poles. I was having an orgasm. My screams were so loud they could wake my neighbours.

He said, "Shut the fuck up", and roughly pulled his cock out of me.

I lost control of my body. The orgasm was too powerful. My body went limp.

He wrapped his hand around my neck and squeezed, saying, "Spread your legs."

I did as he commanded. He was my master at this moment. He commanded my greatest and best orgasms.

He dipped two fingers in my pussy. He moved them in and out. He found my G-spot and massaged it relentlessly. I squirmed under his watchful gaze and skillful foreplay. I couldn't tell how long he was massaging my g-spot before he started to massage my clitoris with his free hand. I had lost all grips on time and reality.

I was living in the moment. I begged him to stop.

I wanted to pee.

He continued to skilfully massage my g-spot. He was relentless in his pursuit of commanding my orgasms. I couldn't hold it any longer. I started to pee. It was spraying on his chest and ruining my bed linens.

I was embarrassed. He was laughing. He enjoyed my discomfort.

He removed his fingers from my vagina slowly while smiling from ear to ear. I thought he was satisfied. He licked his fingers and got on bended knees. He patted my pussy lips lovingly and dived in.

He French-kissed my pussy and then got right back up.

I was sleepy. I fell asleep in a jello heap on the edge of the bed. I slept contently like an over-fed puppy.

The next morning, I woke up and didn't feel the familiar soreness that is usually felt the morning after steamy sex with a "horse-dicker".

My sheets were damp but my body showed no evidence of having been fucked the way I remember.

Oh shit! It was all a dream.

A dream I wouldn't mind becoming a reality.

Chapter 5:
Chyn

Last night, the dreams I had of Kloud had been surreal. I woke up the happiest woman alive, but my bed was empty. I searched my body for proof of the mind-blowing sex that I'd had.

Nope, no evidence there.

I raked my brain but I couldn't remember disabling my alarm system, so it was definitely a dream. For good measure though, I checked my home surveillance and just as I'd thought, it was only a really intense dream that I thoroughly enjoyed. Much as I enjoyed the dream I was annoyed at Kloud for wasting my time. Time is money and money makes me very happy.

Every time Kloud disappointed me I became more determined to win him over. I was a whole clown for that man. God help me.

Since Kloud didn't bother showing up, I needed some head to take the edge off and get me back in relaxation mode. Just so I could focus on making this money, and I knew exactly who to call.

* * *

My fingers clawed at the sheets that were bunched up all around me, as an orgasm tore through my body.

My screams were drowned by the high-pitched sounds of Aidonia playing from the surround sound in my living room.

Jah kept flicking his tongue against my clitoris. Back and forth. Back and forth.

Back and *sweet* forth. Slower then faster. Slower then *faster* still.

He'd inserted two fingers into my vagina inconspicuously. He was using both fingers to stroke my g-spot, prompting my body to betray me involuntarily.

I came long and hard, my body trembled from the intensity of the orgasm. I was vulnerable. He knew I was coming. He continued to lick me. Trying to get me to climax as much as possible.

I pushed his head away from my vagina. It felt ticklish. I was annoyed. I had come to my senses. This wasn't my baby. This wasn't Kloud. I enjoyed cunnilingus from Jah only because I was imagining that he was Kloud.

It only worked long enough for me to orgasm once.

As soon as I come, I come to my senses.

Jah could never sense the shift in my mood, he'd eat my honeypot all day if I allowed it. Shit the way he kept slurping, I'd taste myself to confirm whether or not my pussy was really that sweet.

I mean a bitch ate her pineapples religiously but damn!!!

Chapter 6:
Chyn

Being pretty is overrated in this day and age. It doesn't matter if your pretty is authentic or store-bought. You'll still get used, abused and ghosted. Matter of fact pretty fucking hurts.

Chyn stood in her mirrored bedroom and looked at herself from all angles. She is stacked perfectly with small perky tits, smooth pecan coloured skin, thick pink lips, absolutely no waist, and a pretty face. Shorty has back because her ass jiggles with her every move.

She stared at her reflection and wonder what men thought when they saw her. She is intelligent, has numerous degrees and other accolades, and is independent, got dreams and aspirations that could be inclusive if she found someone special and is not a gold digger by anyone's standard.

Why do men only see her body and not her? Why do men only want to fuck?

She likes Kloud, but he seems preoccupied with someone else. All these other men saw her but she only has eyes for him.

He doesn't text. He doesn't call, except when he wants to fuck. She's a sucker for that man. She's a sucker for that dick. Somehow no matter how much she coaches herself on ways of cussing him out and telling him she's not interested in having sex, the second his number pops up on her Caller ID, her pussy starts dripping.

She hyperventilates at the thought of being in his presence.

Suddenly, her phone rings shaking her from her thoughts. It was a call from Gary. She hissed her teeth and placed the phone right back on the night stand.

She wasn't in the mood to entertain that fool tonight. Placing her manicured feet in her Pink house-slippers, she went downstairs to fetch some wine.

The phone kept ringing. Gary wouldn't stop calling. Chyn was annoyed. She was annoyed that Gary wouldn't stop calling but Kloud didn't call at all.

Having a change of heart, she answered, pretending to yawn. "Hello?"

"What's up shorty? Why I always gotta call ya one hundred times before you pick up?"

"I'm not obligated to answer my phone that *I* pay the bill for, that's why," she retorted. "Anyway, did you call to argue or nah?"

"Ever since I gave you this dick, you've been tripping. I'm trying to help you fix that bitchy attitude of your," he drawled in his lazy tone.

To think he'd get a clue by now. We fucked once and I never once called or texted him after. The sex was trash. He fucked like a monster. There was just nothing seductive about roughly twisting my breast in a clockwise direction like he was trying to pull them from my chest. Let me not even think about how he jammed his fingers into my vagina or how he avoided my clitoris at all costs.

He was a waste of my prowess. I felt sorry for him.

"Pick me up at 9 pm. Ensure you have non-latex Trojan condoms and a bottle," she replied.

She didn't want to be alone with thoughts of Kloud all night. So to avoid the loneliness, she subjected herself to good company and bad sex.

She got dressed in a burgundy No Boundaries dress with stripes at the sides and white converse sneakers. She had perfectly manicured cum white fingernails and toe-nails. She ensured she didn't wear a bra or any panties. She splashed some Gucci *Guilty* cologne on.

The doorbell dinged. He was outside.

I scooped up my iPhone and my keys in my mini- backpack and stepped out. He hugged me and I did a twirl so he could see my entire outfit. He slapped my ass and muttered 'damn' under his breath.

He drove a basic Mark X. Not the ideal car. My Jeep is fatter and more expensive, but I didn't care though. Despite him being a trashy fuck, he was still decent company.

I despised him for not being Kloud. I despised that I was with him right now trying to fill the emptiness that not being with Kloud caused. I wanted to cry despite him chattering away, entertaining me. I compared every man to Kloud. They didn't make me smile the way he did.

Nobody did anything the way he did.

"Are you hungry?" he disrupted my thoughts. He could be such a gentleman.

"I want fries and ice-cream."

He laughed at my choice of food or the lack thereof.

It was heartbreak food, and I was heartbroken over a man that didn't want me.

We drove to a convenience store and he bought what I requested and threw in a bottle of Patron. When we exited the store, I noticed he was driving further away from his house.

"Why are we going in this direction? Isn't your place that way?" Chyn inquired.

"Yea but my girl is home until next month, so we going somewhere nice," he quipped.

I was annoyed and wished I hadn't left my house.

Sigh! It's about to be a long-ass night.

We parked in the hotel's lot and he went to secure the room. I checked my phone for the 100th time. Still no text or call from Kloud.

I powered off my cellphone and decided to make it a good night. The minute I entered the room, I discarded my dress. I sat on the bed in all my naked glory and he peered at me with a smirk on his face.

I wondered briefly about that smirk.
I opened the Patron and drank directly from the bottle, while he rolled some weed.

I powered on the television. A girl was getting fucked on screen. She was mad extra and annoying because the penis was small as fuck and I could literally see the man's penis shrinking with each thrust. I turned off the television.

His phone rang.

"Hey babe!" he answered, upbeat while staring at me. He silently begged me not to talk and I nodded knowingly. I wasn't going to fuck up this man's home because I didn't want him like that.

"I'm out with the boys. I'll be home by midnight. Do you want me to take you something? Ok, I love you too. Squeeze your pussy for me.....love you too... Alright. Later, wifey!" he hurried the conversation.

He placed the phone on the night stand. I took in his attire. He was a skinny nigga. Almost scrawny.

He had donned a navy blue polo shirt with skinny jeans, and paired them with a tan no-brand belt and matching desert *Clarks*.

I wasn't impressed.

Kloud had perfect weight. He wasn't too slim

or stout. He would ensure that his attire made me want to take off my non-existent panties.

I tried to pick up which cologne he was wearing. He must've been wearing some cheap shit cuz I was good at naming men's cologne.

I watched him intently as he lit his weed. He took a pull and coughed. I laughed. *Punk!* I thought.

I lit the additional weed he rolled and alternated between drinking the Patron and smoking the weed.

He placed the lighted weed in the ashtray and went to take a shower.

When he returned from the bathroom, he tried to kiss me. I didn't kiss men I didn't love. I turned away my face.

He kissed all over my neck and with each kiss, I turned my neck. I didn't like the dude like that. Foreplay wasn't necessary.

Fuck me and let's go! I thought, annoyed.

He pinched my nipples and they stood erect under his watchful eyes. He was satisfied. He licked and bit on my nipples relentlessly. It was painful and I didn't enjoy it one bit.

He proceeded to massage my breast roughly. Pulling them in all different directions. A tear fell from my eyes.

I'm hurting myself.

The best way to get over a nigga is to fuck another nigga. Or so I heard.

It's not working. My heart broke even more each time Gary sucked on my nipples. I really wanted to prove to myself that this thing with Kloud was just a stupid crush.

So, I spread my legs and started to play with my pussy.

I closed my eyes. Visions of Kloud overtook my thoughts.

He removed my hands from my pussy and stared at it. My wax grew out so it was now neatly shaved. I opened my legs wider so he could see everything, and closed my eyes, anticipating his next move. I waited for minutes with my eyes closed. My heart beat wildly in my chest. But he didn't touch me.

I half-listened for any movement in the room. There was none. I half opened my eyes and peeped at him.

He already had on a condom. But his dick was limp.

I'm wasn't the play-with-it-until-it-gets-hard kind of a bitch. Hell no!

He grabbed the remote and turned on the television. The room vibrated with moans and groans from the porn actress on the TV.

He then pulled me off the bed and tried to put my arms around his neck.

I removed my hands and said, "If you want to make love go home to wifey. If you wanna fuck, let's do that then."

He nodded and squeezed my ass. I regurgitated a little and almost vomited up the fries I had eaten earlier. I was literally sick to my stomach being in close proximity with this man who wasn't my Kloud.

His dick was still limp. He had his little willie with a condom on beating in his palm. It was hilarious as fuck.

"Gary, lay down a bit cuz you're either tired or too anxious." I hid my laughter.

I scooted over on the bed. He laid down beside me. I turned my head away from him. This felt awkward. I was ready to go home because this was a waste of my evening.

All of a sudden he scrambles off the bed. I turned my head frightened. He held his stomach and vomited all over the bed and floor.

I was in shock. I was embarrassed for him. My nurse instincts kicked in but I didn't want to do or say anything to embarrass him any further. After he finished puking out him soul, he went into the bathroom and closed the door. I remembered my sneakers and went to check if he vomited on them too.

Thank God he didn't fuck up my sneakers. So,

I started to get dressed. He came out of the bathroom with an entire roll of tissue and started to clean his puke off the floor but before he even finished, he started to vomit again.

I was wondering what the fuck he ate. From my knowledge, he only ate some fries, drank half a bottle of magnum tonic wine and smoked half a joint.

Now, I was side-eyeing this bitch.
I was screaming in my mind '*nigga get the fuck up*'.

He proceeded to vomit for three hours on and off.

I was trying to wait out his vomiting spell. Then, I noticed the colour of the vomit moved from bright pink to clear. That meant his stomach was empty now.

I was relieved.

He continued to vomit clear liquid. Once he was through, he knelt on the floor and rest his head on the bed.

At this point I was stunned. This was exactly

how I'd knelt on the floor with my head on the bed, holding my stomach on many nights after Kloud fucked up my guts with his big black pretty dick.

"Gary, it's 2 am in the morning. Let's get me home so you can go home. When you get there, get wifey to make you some tea," I said.

"I don't know why I drank that Magnum. I know I shouldn't have," he replied. "Maybe I really do need some tea or ginger ale."

He threw on his clothes and opened to the door for me to exit.

I declined the drive home. "Go home and get some rest. I'll call a cab."

"I can't leave you here," he replied.

"I'll stay in the room until the cab gets here. Plus I can take care of myself." I pointed my fingers, replicating a gun being fired.

He turned and tried to kiss my cheek with puke on his breath. I stepped away.

"Damn! It's like that?" He sounded hurt.

"I never said I would take care of you. That's

wifey's job," I replied sarcastically.

I walked him to his car and he pulled out a gift-bag which he handed to me. I peeked inside and smiled. He got me my favourite gift; 'twas a bag of money. I was *cheesing*.

He promised to call before he entered his house. I didn't care if he called or not.

I walked out of the hotel's parking lot and caught a cab. Despite him giving me one hundred thousand dollars in a gift bag, he was a wanna-be and a fucking punk. He fucked up my whole night and then left me to find my own ride, with a bag of money.

I sat in the cab and deleted his number. When I got home, I thanked the driver and paid him three times the amount he charged. I then got in, had a shower and powered on my phone. Still…nothing from Kloud.

I remembered singing along with Alkaline's *Company*.

Now, look at my pathetic ass. I fell in love with

someone who'd never belong to me. I tried to cry myself to unconsciousness. But I couldn't fully sleep.

He plagued my thoughts at all times.

Chapter 7:
Chyn

As I sat in my living room with the gift bag that Gary had given me, I realized how empty my life really was.

I had all this money and nobody to share my successes with. Every night while the neighbourhood slept I sat somewhere in my house surrounded by money, liquor, and drugs.

It really was a cold life when you're rich and lonely.

Money doesn't buy happiness.

The harder I searched for "Mr Right", the more he evaded me. The better I looked, the more 'simps' I attracted. The harsh reality was that men were in fact out there. I attracted them like flies but it was hard finding ultimate satisfaction for my palate.

I had a type.

No matter who I dated or what stories I fed them, my body, mind, and vagina seemed to react differently to mysterious men. The mystery just happened to be Virgo men. The ones with sexy lips and white teeth. The ones whose smile was a mixture of innocence and mischievousness.The ones who exuded confidence and commanded attention whenever they entered a room.

Height and weight, average. Beard and tattoo were a given. Swag on point. Cologne kicking. Attitude savage, definitely *not* average.

Oops…I got carried away. I'm sure you understand. Back to the rant!

I'm a spitfire so I require attention and strong leadership. Almost all men are "yes men" except the unique Virgo men. I crave balance as all Libras do but my willpower is stronger than most. Virgo men are willing to say "no" and mean it.

They are always prepared to not be my favourite just for keeping it real, and they are willing and able to challenge my sexual prowess.

Somehow they highlight the wife in me.

So, I become domestic. I do all the washing, cooking, cleaning and uplifting, praying for them…but then they go home to wifey. Nobody has the power to keep me interested except the Virgo man, but I don't seem to have the power to keep *him* interested.

It's all a game. A power struggle.

I'm not willing to fight the battle, I choose to be the side-chick. I know what to expect but I'd never accepted it as my reality. I can never seem to figure out how much to give or how much is too much.

I cry because of loneliness on many nights. Tonight is no different. I'd fallen for less than I truly deserved once again. Kloud would text once in a while to ensure that the link is still intact so that he could fuck on demand. I allow him to do so because, quite frankly, I want to fuck too.

After we fuck, I never want him to leave. I wanna lay up in his arms and tell him about my day.

Never gonna fucking happen!

I pray, though. I pray for his safety so I can continue to think about him and not grieve about him. I pray for his successes because with a dick like that he deserves it. I pray for his health and strength because once he's well, I know I'll get the D once in a while. I pray he never wants because I'll go broke supplying. I pray he never cries because the world will have to deal with my wrath. I pray his wife never reads our messages; I don't want her to leave him because of me. I don't want to win him over by default.

And I pray for his kids born and unborn.

I pray daily for that man. A man that belongs to someone else.

Maybe I'm the toxic one, but I'm loyal. Loyalty begins with yourself. Staying true to one's self and feelings, accepting one's flaws and honing one's skill is the first step to loyalty. You cannot accept someone for who they truly are until you've first accepted yourself.

I've accepted Kloud as being a fuckboy, albeit my fuckboy!

Chapter 8:
Kloud

I couldn't understand why my key didn't work in the door to my house. Neither could I understand why my wife didn't unlock the door so I could get in. I called her phone over and over. I could hear the phone ringing from outside.

I was frustrated. I've had a long day.

"Azuri! Zuri, Zuri? What the fuck is going on?" I demanded an answer.

No answer.

I was outside for hours alternating between drumming on the door and yelling for my wife to open the door.

She was inside, I knew!

She was battling on whether or not she should let me in. I felt her presence on the other side of the door occasionally. She never answered any of my screams though. She held her composure like a champ. She also had me looking like a bitch to my entire neighbourhood.

I didn't care though. She was the woman of my dreams and when all else failed, I needed my wife.

I gave up trying to get inside and sat my ass on the porch. I'd never leave Azuri, not even when she changed the locks on a nigga.

I sat on the porch in the wee hours of the morning, looking at the morning sky. I wondered what had caused the shift in my wife's behaviour. My usually calm wife had practically thrown me out of my house, and without any reason.

I am a great husband to her. While I do my dirt, I ensure that I never bring home any drama. I was confident that she was oblivious to all my extracurricular activities too.

My wife is a Latina. She favoured a young Lauren London. That's how pretty she is.

She has let herself go completely though.

When I first met her, shorty was bad. Four years into the marriage and fatty looks *bad*. I don't care, I love my wife.

This is why I'm sweating and it's cold out here.

I raked over my wife's state of mind until I involuntarily fell asleep.

Click!

I heard front door open. I rubbed the sleep from my eyes and rose to my feet swiftly. My wife stepped out and closed the door behind her. *Wtf!!*

Wowww! Hold up for just a motherfucking second. My WIFE stepped out and closed OUR door behind her, after changing the locks and forcing a nigga to sleep outside.

Something was going on.

Azuri stepped pass me in a black River Island mini-skirt that was buttoned down in the front. I had bought her that skirt about 5 eons ago and couldn't convince her to wear it. She also sported a signature cropped top logo Levi blouse and red and black Jordan Retro 13s. She sported some Gucci shades and a Guess crossbody bag.

She smelled like me too.

Again…*wtf?!*

She wore my signature *Azarro: Wanted* cologne.

Azuri stepped past me…unbothered. She didn't even look my way… Not once.

Something had changed. My wife adored the ground I walked on.

"Zuri, you've had your fun. Tell me what's going on and don't get fucked up," I demanded.

Her reply froze my heart. "*You* don't get fucked up, dear husband," she replied so calmly. "Since you're forcing me to talk to you before I've had my morning coffee, just know I want a divorce.

"A di-," I was about to question but she cut me off.

"A divorce, motherfucker!" she yelled.

My neighbours had by this time started to gather to witness our argument.

"I know about *all* your affairs. I know that you got fired from your job almost 7 months ago and I also know that you are a drug dealer and a fucking thief. I know that you are under investigation for money-laundering and I *know* that you got a mistress and a fucking baby right across the street." By this time, she was crying.

I scooped her up effortlessly while she kicked and screamed. I pulled the keys off her skirt and opened our door. I walked to the living room and placed her on the couch.

The minute I put her down, she slapped the fuck out of me.

"What I don't fucking know is when you were going to tell me all of this? See, I married you for better or for worse and would've stuck with you through anything! Just *not* two kids and a mistress across the street with a White House and a picket garden fence. Just sign the papers, pack your shit and be gone punk."

She knew everything. I couldn't deny any of it because it was all the truth. But how did she find out?

I looked in her eyes and I didn't see the innocence I once saw. Instead, it was replaced with disappointment and hurt.

I wouldn't argue. I'll go for now, because I never wanted to see my wife cry and I never wanted see that look in her eyes.

So, I kissed her cheek and walked out the door.

"Take care, Zuri. I love you ma and I will fix this even if it's one day before I die."

I hurriedly walked to my car with my heart constricting in my chest and my eyes watering.

Men don't cry, I tried to remind myself.

I took out my phone and called Chyn. She would rescue me because she was desperate for this dick.

Chapter 9:
Chyn

I rose at 6 am on Valentine's Day. I checked my phone... No notifications. This was the life of a single person. I wouldn't dwell on my singleness today. There's money to be made.

I decided to go with the flow of the day. I did my morning routine and was ready to go in no time. I massaged my body with Gucci Premiere body lotion and sprayed myself with the matching perfume. I rummaged through my closet and decided to wear a white mesh teddy-bear bodysuit and some red booty shorts.

I made it a rule that my shoes should match my top at all times. Needless to say, I decided to wear my white cut-away Bridget sandals. I looked at myself from all angles throughout my mirrored room and I looked edible even to me. My eyes caught the glare from my nipple rings.

Diamonds are a girl's best friend lol.

My wet and wave tresses were popping. I wore some lip-gloss and no make-up.

I taped my holster around my left thigh and secured my baby.

I drove my Jeep out of the garage and was on my way to the warehouse. I turned the stereo all the way up as I listened to Offset and Cardi B's song *Clout* all way to the warehouse.

Our newest warehouse was in the middle of nowhere. It was an old sugar factory that I purchased to start another strip-club. It was currently being used for all of our meetings. I had twelve chicks that worked under my supervision, and I only employed pretty bitches.

They made enough money, so they bought the bodies to go with their faces. I had twelve bad bitches at my beck and call. They all had heart and were ready to blast at all times.

I walked through the door with my pink Bejeweled *Smith & Wesson* Shield 9mm in my hand.

I pointed it toward the thirteenth bitch that sat in my warehouse. I didn't know her and she didn't know me. She heard of me though, I was sure.

Kat stood with her gun pointed at me and eleven other guns pointed at both her and the new girl.

Nobody moved for a millisecond and I knew, they weren't getting soft. I smiled to myself.

I lowered my gun and laughed. Everyone else lowered their guns and laughed along with me except the new girl. She seemed uncomfortable.

"Boss, this is Zuri. She's the girl I was telling you about. Yeah, she's solid," Kat spoke up.

"Ahhh, she's solid. Alright. But can she shoot?" I asked, amazed.

I already had the 411 on the new recruit, though. She was Kloud's wifey. I did a little research on the man I'd fallen for and it turned out he was married as fuck. I wasn't worried, though.

What Chyn wanted, Chyn got. No cap.

I'd hand-picked Azuri and sent Kat to

befriend her. Kat was the friendliest of my girls and could charm an angry lion. I'd already briefed the girls that I needed two new chicks and that I picked one myself so that they wouldn't find the addition strange.

I never divulged the reason I'd handpicked Azuri, though. I needed her close.

Keep your friends close and your enemies even closer.

While Azuri ran the streets for me, I'd keep her husband busy. No one would be the wiser. None of these bitches knew where I really lived and I never shared my personal business. They thought I was their friend and not just the bitch who wrote their check.

Their bad. I'm a one-woman army.

Don't get me wrong, I'd never do any snake shit or anything to hurt them but I'd never trust any of them with the full details of my life. That's how bosses get killed.

So… I allowed Azuri to introduce herself. She ends up telling us about her life and her no-good husband. She told us how she came from a wealthy family, how her father tried to control her every move and every decision.

She even explained how she found out about her husband's cheating, pushing drugs and how he stole millions of dollars from his company and was suspended, pending an investigation.

She even broke down in front of us. While the other ladies consoled her, I'd already concluded that she was going to be the team's weakest link. She talked too much and trusted too easily, albeit I had already known since I was the one who sent Kat to befriend her.

I told them to suit up as we were about to go to our makeshift gun range in the back. I knew Azuri was cute. I knew she was way too friendly and her tongue was loose. But I wanted to know if the bitch could shoot.

We let her take the first shot.

Pow! Bull's eye.

I took note of her posture and the way she

held her gun. This bitch told us everything about herself except how experienced she was with handling guns.

Why did she hide that piece of information?

* * *

We had a good day today and I learned more details about Azuri's personal life than a PI could provide. I was intrigued. She was cute, had a body to die for and was educated as fuck. So why did her husband cheat?

More importantly, why did her husband *to this day* not admit he was even in a relationship? I wondered but not enough to stop me from excusing myself and calling her husband.

I had made Valentine's Day plans with Kloud. I would be meeting him in thirty minutes at the barbershop downtown.

I left the warehouse before all the other girls and sped to meet Azuri's husband--*my man*. I was there in under fifteen minutes and parked on the curb while I texted to tell him that I was outside.

He swaggered outside with a fresh fade and I got wet instantly. He saw the Jeep and walked towards it.

I stepped out of the driver seat and hugged him. He hugged me back and squeezed my ass. I kissed his lips and smiled.

I was happy to see him. He initiated the second kiss by pushing his tongue in my mouth, and I sucked on it for a little and bit his lips gently. I told him to drive as I walked around to the passenger's side.

He was wearing a black slim-fit knee-length distressed jeans with a matching graphic T-shirt to match. The entire fit was from Armani Exchange and he had the matching belt with signature AX buckle.

He wore black Balenciaga sneakers and I was mesmerized. I needed to get home and fuck this man.

I calculated that it would be an approximate

twenty-five minutes drive to my house, give or take.

I started to touch his leg as he drove off. He adjusted my stereo to his liking and plugged in his iPhone and ironically "Secret" by Ann-Marie was playing.

I sang along while I gyrated in my seat.

He side-eyed me and said, "Shorty, stop twerking in that seat. Save all that twerking till we get in."

I didn't have a comeback so I scooted closer to him and showered kisses over his face and ears. I licked his ear lobes seductively before inserting my tongue.

He removed one of his hands from the steering wheel and hugged my body to him while I assaulted his ears with my tongue. I could only hope he paid attention to the road. I continued to suckle on his ears while I used my hands to feel for his dick in his pants.

I removed his hand from my body and crawled over to the driver's side. There was enough space to accommodate my body. I hurriedly unbuckled his belt and opened the buttons on his pants. I released his dick from its confinement.

I licked my lips. His penis was the most beautiful penis I'd ever seen. It was pure dark chocolate. While I wanted to taste him badly, I took a minute to admire his penis and heightened his anticipation. His penis had lots of veins. It was both long, fat and the tip was shaped like the perfect mushroom.

After today I'm becoming a vegetarian, I thought.

I rubbed his dick up and down between my fingers and spit on the tip. I massaged my spit on his penis in a swift motion. I took both his balls in my mouth and hummed gently.

I felt the Jeep jerk.

I spit them out and took them in again. I repeated the humming. While rubbing his length with my fingers, I spit his balls out ensuring that they were wet from my spit. Most men liked it nasty and I was just the right bitch.

I licked up and down his length at my own pace and closed my eyes, finding my focus within. I then covered the head of his penis with my mouth and pulled like a vacuum. I bobbed my head up and down while gently stroking his cock. He was moaning and groaning just the way I liked.

I pulled his dick all the way down my throat so that it touched my tonsils and held it steady while quickly and silently repeating the twenty-third Psalm.

He went wild with trying to fuck my mouth but I held steady with his dick on my tonsil until I finished all the verses. Then I allowed him to fucked my mouth for a bit before I retook control.

I sucked and licked and rolled and hummed, alternating all the moves. He kept weaving the Jeep like a drunken driver.

I felt his dick swell bigger in my mouth and I removed it. I spit on his dick and licked it clean. After cleansing his penis, I placed it in the crevice of my jaw and sucked until I felt him trembled and saw the goosebumps on his legs. I knew he was about to orgasm, so I removed his penis from my mouth and pumped it a few times. His semen spilled all over my face, neck, and breast. I kept pumping and pumping, and he took his hands from the steering wheel and tried to pry my fingers from his penis. I defied him because I had leverage.

I place his lucid penis back inside my mouth and sucked it until it was once again fully erect.

"Fuck," he whispered.

I crawled back over to the passenger side. My face and chest were still splattered with semen. He took his eyes from the road for a split second to peer at me. I used one perfectly manicured finger to wipe the sperm from my chest directly onto my tongue seductively. I sucked on my finger, moaned and swallowed.

I smiled and he promised to make babies when we reached my crib. I tuned him out and took up my phone. I took a selfie of myself for my memories.

I never liked sucking dick before but I definitely was rethinking my position on the entire dick sucking thing. If I could suck his dick like this twice a day I'd never need to have sex again. It was too satisfying watching his many fuck faces.

I might have to kill his wife and marry the nigga.

From this day forth, without his knowledge, his dick belonged to me.

Chapter 10:
Chyn

These days I'm always smiling. I go to sleep with a smile and I wake up every morning with a smile. I silently pray that God preserves my happiness because sometimes I can feel the guilt trying to creep in. Sometimes I would hear my mother's voice in my head warning me, *'A home built on another woman's tears won't last.'*

I couldn't turn back now, but I could do everything in my power to keep this man in my home, in my bed, in my vagina and in my heart.

We'd been having sex around the clock. If he smiled, I
Would suck his dick. If he got mad, I ride his dick. But most importantly, I've been getting to know him; to *really* know him. I truly loved this man.

I loved this man unconditionally. I mean, you know you're in love when you're out shopping for yourself and you end up stopping to get him gifts too. Like, *this shirt would look good on bae* and *this pair of pants is going to go perfectly with the shirt.* Before you know, it your shopping spree becomes a "spoiling bae" day.

You know you're in love when you're out in the streets and you compare every guy you meet to him. And you *definitely* know you're in love when nobody measures up after all the comparisons. You know you're in love when he's in bed next to you and you lay there and watch him sleep. And you're definitely in love when you pray for him while he sleeps next to you.

Yes, I've got it bad.

Sigh.

Kloud has been staying at my place for months on end. He stays here all day everyday, even while I comb the streets trying to make some money. I pay the bills. I buy the food. I do everything up in this bitch while this nigga lies on my couch *all* fucking day.

I mean, love him. His penis is to die for but I'm getting fucking annoyed. I'm going to ose these feelings real quick. *Please*, Dear God, make him have some go-hard in his blood and a heart in his chest.

Impulsively, I walked into my house and pulled my gun out my holster. I took it off safety and I aimed it towards the couch. I didn't even think twice because I just knew that was where this motherfucking nigga would be sprawled out eating my food like a bitch.

But I was in for a rude awakening....

I heard a click behind me. I smelled his essence instantly. Kloud stood behind me with a gun pointed at my head whilst my gun pointed towards the empty couch.

"Bitch, why are you trying to kill me?" he barked to the back of my head.

I didn't move at all. Instead, I laughed loudly and sinisterly.

"If I wanted to kill you, you'd be dead. Look,

I'm going to put my gun in its place and I'm going to sit on the couch. Join me!" Chyn replied authoritatively.

She stuck her gun in its place and walked to the couch. She propped down and waited for him to join her. When he did, she laid out to him that he needed to get a job in order to help pay the bills. She also let him know that as his fucking skills were, he needed to become the head of the household or get out her house.

He said he'd be leaving soon.

But I knew he had some money. He wasn't broke by anyone's standard. He still paid the bills at Azuri's house. I knew this because she continuously boasted about it to us.

I was most men's dream come true, except Kloud's.

No matter what I did for him or to him. He only yearned for Azuri's love and forgiveness. He regularly sneaked out of my bed to send her messages or demand that she answer his calls. I knew because she boasted about it. I also recently had his phone wired and installed a tracking system on his car.

I know when he leaves my house ad when he returns, but I don't make him any wiser. I even track his iPhone from my phone.

His smiles didn't reach his eyes anymore. His hard- earned money was never spent on me or in my house. It was all wired to her accounts and all her bills stayed paid.

You just can't compete with the woman a man loves. She has his heart, I've got his body parts.

Chapter 11: Kloud

I had set up a camera in my living room without letting Azuri know it.

It wasn't to spy on her or anything. I was just in some deep shit that I'd been hiding from my wife. I just wanted her to be safe at all times. The camera had come in handy these days. It was the only way to see my wife's beautiful face.

The minute Chyn walked out the door, I opened the surveillance app and reviewed footage from my home. Today, I saw my wife crying for hours on end and as a man, it shattered my heart into pieces. She was innocent in everything that was been happening. In my quest to protect and provide for my wife, I grew greedy and fucked up the best thing I'd ever had.

I remember she was a sheltered rich kid who got whatever her heart desired and I was a broke orphan who worked part-time with the cleaning company that her father had hired.

She talked to me with respect. She pulled me from the streets and showed me another way of life. We fostered a close friendship until the day she cried on my shoulder that her father was too controlling and didn't approve of the friendship.

I had vowed that I would work hard and gain some money, some status and her father's respect so that she could love us both in harmony.

But I had ended up impregnating her when we were both seventeen years old and she chose me over her dad and an abortion. She left her rich family, bright future and comfortable home to weather the storms of life with me.

But unfortunately, she'd suffered a stillbirth. To this day, she is still broken. I'd broken all the promises that I'd made to my wife, but I did it all so that she could regain her status and be proud to wear my name. I realized way too late that nothing much mattered to her except my love.

I tried calling my wife many times per day and I watched many times on the camera as she declined my calls.

Dear God, I don't know how to fix this. Please touch my Zuri's heart with your loving hands. Open her heart, oh Lord, and make her like You who forgives seventy times seven. Selah!

I closed the surveillance app and rested my head on the arm of the couch. I thought of Chyn. I respected her. She worked hard and was independent. I see all her awards of recognition plastered on the walls in different sections of her home, but I'm yet to see her getting ready for a 9-5 job.

She's clearly well off because she lives in an upper-class neighbourhood, wears expensive clothes and spares no expense when she goes shopping for herself or me.

She was no Azuri. My wifey would never even attempt to buy a man. Azuri helps to build me, she'd never try to buy me. I've gotta be forever grateful.

Everything I know, I picked up from the streets and I seriously believe in the idea: *'give a man a fish, and you feed him for a day. Teach a man to fish, and you feed him for a lifetime'* .

Azuri was the wifey type while bitches like Chyn, you just fuck and kept it moving. Chyn tries to be the best woman she can possibly be. She was a good woman too, just not for me. I never wanted a gangster type of woman. I wanted someone who I can love and protect. Someone who makes me feel wanted and appreciated for small gestures. Chyn was the new-aged independent, the "I can do it on my own" type.

If I should ever settle for her, I would be smacking her up and down the house every day trying to get her to
act right.

I would peep her walking around everywhere with her gun. I still couldn't understand why a pretty bitch like Chyn felt the need to be toting guns around town.

I didn't know and I pray I never found out too.

I was only staying here until I got my wife back. Chyn was just a tight pussy and a wet mouth. Every day after she left the house, I'd drive out right after. I ensured to ride around the block to see if I'd get lucky and Azuri would take me back.

After my stressful days out in the streets trying to earn enough money to pay the bills at home, I'd always walk right back into Chyn's house and redress in the same clothing I was in when she left. Whenever I heard the alarm being deactivated, I'd pretend to be engrossed in a movie or video game. I would never make Chyn any wiser.

Suddenly, I heard like something was shaking. I was on high alert.

It stopped.

I heard the shaking again. I grabbed my gun

from under the couch and crept into the kitchen where the sound was coming from.

I peeped her phone on the counter. I peeped a 'Gary' calling from the caller ID but the phone stopped vibrating the second I picked it up.

I placed it back down and turned to walk away. It started vibrating again. 'Gerald' was calling. I watched it until it stopped ringing. It immediately rang again.

Chyn had eighty missed calls, five hundred and sixty-six text messages, one thousand and one WhatsApp messages, ten notifications from Instagram, two from Twitter and fifteen Snapchat notifications.

What the fuck was this bitch on?

She's antisocial, nobody visits here. Nobody calls the house phone…and thinking of it, I've never even seen her speaking on her cell before or heard it ringing or vibrating until today.

Something is not right!

I put the phone back where it was and made a

mental note to watch her more keenly…

Since I was already in the kitchen, I decided to grab some food. I was tired of take-out and frozen pizza. Might as well cook us some dinner.

Surprisingly, the fridge is always fully stacked even though Chyn barely cooked. I've never ventured to the pantry though so I pulled open the cabinet and I saw a black handle…

Wait….was that a fucking gun?

I pulled it out. It was a Glock 45. *Wtf* was this chick on?

I opened all the cabinet doors and guns were behind every single one of them.

I closed all the doors and was walking back to my spot on the couch. I turned the corner and I saw Chyn taking her bejeweled gun off safety.

The bitch was pointing her gun towards where I would normally be sitting.

I was shocked for a second. Why would Chyn want to shoot me?

I crossed the hallway and stood behind her

with my own gun pointed to her head, while her gun pointed at the empty couch.

"Bitch, why are you trying to kill me?' I barked to the back of my head.

She didn't move at all.

"If I wanted to kill you, you'd be dead," she said. "I'm going to put my gun in its place and I'm going to sit on the couch. Join me!"

She said it so matter-of-factly.

She then stuck her gun in its place and walked to the couch, propped down and waited for me to join her…and I followed like a sick puppy. These days she had started to boss up on me and it turns me on just a little.

When I'd recovered from the shock of her pulling her gun on me, she laid out to me that I needed a job to help pay the bills and pull my weight around her house.   She even talked about how greatly I fucked her but that I also needed to be the head of the household or get out.

I was a little embarrassed; she had made me

feel less of a man. I was also reminiscent of when I couldn't take care of or provide for Azuri.

So, I answered and told Chyn that I'd be leaving soon.

Who the fuck did Chyn think she was, anyway? Here she was, setting rules as if she was my wife. I needed to tell her that I had no Mom and already had a Mrs. But that would only open a whole different can of worms because all the time that we'd been together, I'd never told her that I wasn't single.

I couldn't change my tune now plus, as bossed-up as Chyn was, I could almost guarantee that she'd flip the fuck out. She wasn't the type to knowingly play second best.

I'd better leave Chyn's house soon before I broke her fucking neck and threw her to the sharks. At this point, I just needed my kind-hearted wife to calm my raging spirit.

Chapter 12:
Katura

I'm Katura. Everybody calls me Kat.

I don't know how to introduce myself or how to talk about me exactly. I've not had my own identity in many years. I can go on and on about my boss Chyn or the Money Bag Bitches for hours but I don't know shit about myself really. I'd lost my identity by running in a pack for most of my life.

I thought about my identity as my friend Zuri went on and on about I don't know what. I tuned her out. She was the nicest human being alive but she talked too fucking much. I loved my peace and sometimes I grew annoyed at her and her chattering.

I didn't know what the boss lady had up her

sleeves. Something felt off about the way she sent me to befriend Azuri. We didn't befriend people. We shoot first and asked questions later in the kind of business we're in. I wasn't going to ask any questions regarding my boss's decision to expand though. There was always a method to her madness.

The reason didn't concern me.

Azuri was so pretty and educated and had the ability to do anything she wanted to do with her life. I wasn't jealous or anything but I felt like she had her entire life ahead of her and was wasting it away crying over a damn man.

We'd been friends from the day I met her in the book store. She was the quiet, homely type that would prefer to stay home with a novel and some wine. I wish my life would be as simple as hers someday, but this is the life I'd chosen and I just got to push it to the limit. No one could get out until or unless Chyn felt like retiring. And with the amount of money and power she had, she wasn't going anywhere any time soon.

Most days, I couldn't bear hearing my phone ring. It symbolized that there was more money to make or people to kill. Some days, it meant that I would have to fuck some random nigga and take his shit. I wasn't even into men like that.

Azuri... I'm into her.

Nobody on my team knew that I was secretly living a lesbian life and the fact that Chyn sent me to befriend Azuri did me no favours.

Chyn had found out that Zuri spent most of her time either volunteering at the local orphanage or at the library reading all kinds of books. She was easy to stalk. I basically learnt her routine and started showing up at places that she was scheduled to be. I bumped into her while she tried to check out at the library with some books that she was borrowing for the week. From there, we became friends.

Some days, Azuri and I would spend hours on the phone talking about all kinds of random stuff. Other days, we went shopping or did sleepovers.

Unbeknownst to me, I was her only friend. What she didn't know though is that I didn't need or want any new friends. What I needed was for her to stop prancing around my house in those booty shorts with her fat ass on display. I needed for her to just stop acting clueless and let me taste her pussy.

I tried to keep my cool around Zuri because even though she decided to hang with me and my team, I felt like she was just doing it for the excitement. If it turned out that was the case, when shit hit the fan she would try to either snitch or leave. No one left the team except in a fucking body-bag. That was law.

Chyn was the only boss with a dozen right hands.

I liked Azuri and wished she hadn't joined the crew. And if given the chance, I'd lick her pussy till she no longer
knew she had one. However, my loyalty stood with
Chyn. Forever.

She took a chance on me, a chance no one else cared enough to take.

I had been forced into prostitution by an old nigga who I'd thought was going to rescue me from poverty. Instead, he abused me physically and emotionally every chance he got. I never saw a dime from all the dirty cocks I sucked or fucked.

I had hidden the cash I'd made on the day Chyn had stepped out of her car and rescued me. I'd worked six 'johns' and hid the money because I'd been planning my escape. He'd thought that I was lying about business being slow and started beating my ass like I was a man in the streets.

Chyn had been driving a BMW at the time. She'd pulled up, stopped on the curb and told him she needed my services. I was allowed to enter her car. Once I got in, she shouted for me to shut the fuck up with the crying and feeling sorry for myself. Told me I'd better find a way to boss up.

She was beautiful and commanded my attention so it wasn't hard for me to listen. She put her gun in my hand plus some money, told me to kill Joe and then be at an address by 10 pm if I wanted a new life.

That was the test.

I'd never used a gun before but I figured it out. He was dead in the middle of the streets two hours after she drove off, and I was at the address three hours before I was supposed to be.

She helped me clean my bruises and gave me room and board. I was never forced to join the team. I chose my path because of my loyalty towards her.

When it came on to Chyn, I would fuck shit up without thinking twice.

Chapter 13:
Azuri

I'm the infamous Azuri. Y'all know so much about me and may have already formed opinions but nobody that who has spoken about me truly knows me.

I'm Azuri de la Velasquez RN, Esq, daughter of the ruthless assassin and drug lord, Velasquez. My father never wanted a daughter, he wanted a son to carry on his name and inherit his drug and cartel legacy after he died.

I'm sick of been treated like a delicate flower who needs to be protected from the world. I'm a genuinely nice person with a good heart but that doesn't mean that I won't fuck shit up if needs be.

No one even knew that my father had children, least of all a daughter. He preferred it that way. He never wanted me to be used as leverage in dirty negotiations or any of his drug wars. I understood from a young age to be present but stay out of his way. My father loves me, I never doubted his love. He did his best to protect me, I was sure. He wanted the best for me like any loving parent would want for their child. The problem was the way he would always approach stuff.

My dad ran shit in the streets. I found that out at a very young age. I'd just wanted him to be a normal dad. Instead, he'd always been so demanding of me. He demanded me to be the best at everything I did, and I was. Then he demanded that I kept only a certain type of friends. He basically made demands on my entire life.

But I idolized my dad. I worshipped the ground he walked on, but he broke me down every chance he got. I was never good enough. He'd say he was proud of me for all my accomplishments but at the same time demanded more.

I had lived my entire life in a mansion on the outskirts of Beverley Hills. I had no neighbours.

The closest estate had six miles away from us. I had private tutors and my friends were cousins or the staff members' kids until I'd been shipped off to boarding school.

While I was at school, I'd raised hell and had gotten expelled. My dad had no choice but to enroll me in a local private school, where I came home every day after dismissal. He was home to greet me daily after school and helped with my homework and stuff. We had gotten close.

We drifted apart again when I entered my teenage years and became close friends with Kloud. Kloud had been a new employee at the time. He worked part-time to save up enough money for college.

My father saw the budding friendship and thought nothing of it until Kloud started bringing me roses and stuff. He fired him and forbade me from seeing him. I defied my father because every chance I got, I ran away from home and spent time with Kloud. After being fired, he resorted to stealing cars, robbing stores and doing anything to get by. That didn't affect our relationship though, because we'd grown closer than ever and I'd had no intention of letting him go.

I never listened to my dad's advice at all because I'd thought Kloud was going to be my knight in shining armour.

Look at us now.

I got pregnant at 17 years old. My dad threw me out and disowned me so I ended up moving into a dilapidated old building with Kloud. I never got discouraged though. I had to get it out of the mud. What my father didn't know was: what didn't kill you would always make you stronger.

I remember being stressed out for months on end. I loved my dad, I truly did but I had to live my life. I had to do what made me happy and I had to have Kloud. It wasn't an easy choice to choose Kloud but it was the right thing to do. I even cried myself to sleep many nights. I missed my dad and Kloud couldn't always console me.

I lost our baby eventually and I've been a broken woman ever since.

I grew tired of sitting in an old broken down home staring at the walls while Kloud was out all day and night between schooling and hustling.

So I snuck into my father's house without Kloud even knowing and I hacked my dad's private accounts. I wired myself five million dollars. I ultimately "sponsored" the scholarship that Kloud was awarded. He got a full ride through college as well as a housing grant.

The money I stole upgraded our status from an old house to an apartment. I got a computer and I took online classes. I had a double major in Law and Nursing.

But love would break the strongest of women. It will tear you down until you become a shell of yourself. I lost my life as I knew it years ago because I needed Kloud's love. And now, *again*, my world was in chaos because I loved him.

But I was just now realizing that Kloud had

always been the wrong man.

The right man would not bring pain and heartache. He would bring laughter and good fortune. Kloud had many women and baby mammas around town. The most painful part of it was that he never told me. I loved kids. I'd have taken them all in.

And it had become annoying that everyone thought that I was some sort of fool.

The longest alive will live to see the most.

Kloud tried calling me numerous times each day and stalking me at other times. But I'm never going back to him. I had done all I'd done for him because I loved him and genuinely thought he loved me. In my mind, I made an investment in our future. But I hated disloyalty and I'd never forgive him. We would never, ever be one again.

I hated men. All they did was disappoint.

Kat has been my friend for a couple of months now. She's been helping me to heal. She ensures that I get out of the house a lot. She opens doors for me and allows me to enter before she does. She sends me sunflowers to brighten my day when she has to work and can't be on the phone, and she looks at me like I'm the most beautiful girl in the world.

I've tried men and all they do is disappoint so I'm willing to try women because all the women I've ever known are so loving and gentle.

My phone rang, jerking me from my thoughts. I took it off the night stand and declined Kloud's call.

I then removed the robe that I was wearing, opened my legs and took a photo of my fat pretty pussy and sent it to Katura with the caption: *eat her!!!*

Kat responded instantly with the tongue emoji: *'I'm on my way'*.

I'd always known she was a fucking lesbian. She always said she was single. *Single my ass.*

I responded: *'lol wrong person, you shouldn't have gotten that'*.

'Lol ok. I'm on my way still.'

She pulled up about fifteen mins later with pizza and a bottle of Patron.

We ate and chatted while the movie played.

We'd drunk half the bottle of Patron and was talking a whole lot of shit. I started to feel extremely hot so I took off my blouse and sat back on the couch next to Kat in just my panties and bra.

She kept staring at me so I told her to stop. She got up from the couch and kissed me. I was caught a bit off-guard but I kissed her back.

I felt a shift in the earth.

This must be what I've been missing.

Kat and I kissed for what seemed like an eternity. She kissed all over my face neck, ears, breasts. She ensured that I was fully aroused. My entire body tingled from all her kisses. My boobs were tender from all the sucking and licking and my panties were soaking wet. Kat touched, kissed and licked everywhere except my pussy.

She then opened my legs while I sat on the couch and bent in front of me. I was still wearing my pink mesh panties. She moved my panties to the side and rubbed my clitoris with her fingers. I moaned softly. She started to lap up my juices like a hungry cat drinking some milk.

I pulled my gun from beneath the seating of the couch while she licked and I shot her in the head. She suckled on my clitoris for a brief second longer before she fell over on the floor.

I looked at her and back at the gun as a smile crossed my face.

See…Kat was fake. Something was off about the bitch. I didn't know what it was or who sent her and frankly, I didn't care. She's dead so whoever sent her will come them self and I will be prepared.

I'm wasn't going to get deceived again. Kloud was the last straw. I'd be the one doing the deceiving from now on.

I fucked up my house. I turned over furniture and broke a lot of my nice china cutlery. I thought about that bomb head I was about to receive from Kat before I killed her and I started to cry.

I called Chyn while crying and explained to her frantically how Kat got killed in my house during an home invasion.

If these ladies were after me, they'd surely show their cards after tonight. Kat was nice, but the nicest people often became casualties of war.

Let the fucking show begin.

Chapter 14:
Chyn

"What the fuck?" I must be hearing shit.

Kat was dead, Azuri confirmed.

This didn't make sense. I tried racking my brain to remember any current beef we could have had but the streets had been uneventful for awhile. No flare ups. No take over attempts. Nothing.

I clicked to record the call. I had to keep a level head while I listened to Azuri's account of what had happened. She rambled on frantically trying to get every word out.

I was silent on the line while I listened. I told her not to call the cops. The last thing we needed was the heat
from any investigations.

Kat was my gem. I couldn't believe she was

dead.

After listening to Azuri's explanation, I sent a group message from my business phone to let everyone know what was happening. They were instructed to close all shops and move the products to the underground safes, then meet up at the new warehouse.

I swerved in the middle of the road and drove to Azuri's house.

Shit!

Her driveway was lined with cars. The entire fucking street looked busy. I jumped out of the car before I was fully parked and scanned the area briefly.

All these cars were familiar.

I was about to kill all these stupid bitches on my team! The entire Moneybag clan was parked in front of Azuri's house after I specifically told them to close up the shops and stay on standby at the warehouse.

I knocked on Azuri's door and I knew

Something wasn't right. She said there had been a home invasion. Did the thief knock on her front door too? There wasn't any signs of forced entry.

Jazzie opened the door and hugged me immediately. She cried so hysterically. These ladies were here for answers and so was I. So I decided not to go the fuck off on them.

I pushed the fact that all eleven of them defied my orders to the back of my mind. If my money was short later down the line, there was going to be hell to pay.

I stepped through the door and scanned the area. Kat was still slumped over the coffee table.

My heart dropped to my stomach and did flips. I never knew how much I loved Katura until today. I've seen many dead bodies in my lifetime, and I'm sure Kat's won't be the last, but for some reason I couldn't control the tears.

I couldn't probe Azuri about her death with her body laying just a few feet away.

I took my phone from my pocket with my

fingers shaking badly and dialed for the cleaners. We had to get rid of her body. Kat knew we loved her and that she had a family in us but in this business, we didn't always get to pay our last respects via funerals. Sometimes we had to leave a dead body in the streets and move along.

The cleaners worked their magic on Azuri's house. All evidence of the invasion and of Kat's blood and ultimate death were gone.

Following that horrific incident, we didn't work for a month. The streets were closed. Pockets were dry. Fiends were feening. We terrorized the blocks. We even paid the talkers, and the streets were silent.

Nobody knew who touched Kat except the person who did it. The streets would remain closed. Families were going to die from hunger until we got the information that we needed. Katura's death had to be avenged.

By this time, I'd reverted to smoking weed. Every single time I closed my eyes, I would see

Kat's lifeless body slumped over Azuri's coffee table. Something just didn't feel right.

I placed my joint in the ashtray at my feet, then scrolled through my phone looking at pictures of Kat smiling to put my mind at ease. She was a fire-cracker and she was always strapped and ready to shoot. Kat was a trigger-happy bitch.

How the fuck did she die in a stupid home invasion was the question I kept asking myself. Kat sat with her gun in her lap at all times and Azuri was supposed to be carrying too. How did they get robbed? How did Kat get killed…and the man escaped unscathed?

I scrolled to my voice-recorder and played the clip of Azuri crying and explaining how Kat died.

I listened to it ten times.

She's lying.

She told the story differently the third time around.

Come to think of it, she had seemed to be

observing our reaction to Kat's death when we were all at her house. She was entertaining us like she was hosting a party or something, and she had her gun under the seat of the couch when the cleaners came.

If they were instructed to sit on the couch by the man, while he searched the drawers that were *behind* the couch, how did Kat not reach for her gun that was in her holster on her hip? How did Azuri not reach for her gun that was right there beneath the couch?

Whoever entered the house, they must have both trusted the person. Otherwise Kat would have been the one shooting first. The only explanation was that Azuri must have set Kat up to die somehow.

The question though was…why?

I tried my hardest to remember every detail from the day of Kat's death. I scanned my brain.

Why didn't Azuri tell us that she had a camera in her home?

Speaking of that, I pulled up my surveillance cameras. I hadn't checked them in a month. I was in a bad place.

I secured my earphones in my ears. Kloud had just walked pass me to the kitchen. I didn't need him eaves-dropping on my surveillance.

I pulled up all the safe houses where my products were being kept. Everything seemed normal.

I pulled up my house. *Kloud is one sneaky motherfucker*, I thought.

He'd been leaving the house every day right after I did, only returning home right before I did. He'd then wash the clothes he'd been wearing on the streets and I was never made the wiser.

I watched the footage, amazed. He knew about the guns that were placed strategically all over the house.

He knew a lot and he never mentioned a thing.

That sneaky motherfucker!

Something then caught my eye from the footage.

Kloud placed his phone on the couch and went to the bathroom.

Suddenly, I heard something like Azuri's laughter.

I paused the footage. If he was watching some freaky video, I was marching up those stairs and shooting him to death today.

Kloud lived, ate and shit here. He paid no bills. If he was still fucking with Azuri, then all bets were off. They were both going to die tonight.

I sighed and hit the pay button.

Kloud had set up video surveillance in Azuri's house.

If he has the surveillance, then he knows that I know about his wife. He also knows what went down in that house on the day Katura died…

Bingo! I was about to find out too.

Chapter 15:
Kloud

I've not been able to sleep well for the past month because Chyn has been on edge. She's been cussing and fussing and throwing furniture my way all month. I wasn't allowed to talk in this house. We lived in total silence. She doesn't even want to hear a sound coming from the TV.

Occasionally, if she was high enough or tipsy enough she'd stroll into the room butt-naked and straddle me. She would ride me until she climaxed and then leave the room the same way that she entered.

Silently.

Or she'd enter the room and assume the position by bending all the way over with the perfect arch in her back and waited for me to enter her from behind. She didn't make a sound, not even when I entered her. And trust, my dick was in no way small, by any means.

Sometimes I purposefully hammered into her just so she'd moan. Still, the bitch didn't make a sound.

Fucking her just wasn't the same, but she arguably has the tightest, wettest, fattest and best pussy in the world.
I mean, I love my wife. I'd die for my wife but this dick... it's all Chyn's.

She had written her name all over it with her tight pussy and deep throat! Just thinking of her made my dick misbehave!

My wife doesn't answer her phone anymore. She used to answer and say some slick shit. These days, she seems to have me on her cellphone block-list.

None of these bitches were acting right. A nigga was stressed the fuck out!

I opened my surveillance app on my iPhone and pulled up the perimeter of my house. There was an unmarked van across the street from my house. Goosebumps formed along my arms.

Are these men watching my house to see if I'd show up? *Goddamn it, my wife was in danger!*

I rewound the footage to see how long they'd been watching my house. I rewound it to three months prior.

Nothing.

I opened the screen to preview each month at the same time, then I opened January's surveillance.

I saw a car pull up and a female exited. I saw her watching a movie and laughing with my wife. It was good to see that my wife had found herself a friend. It still broke my heart though to know that my wife never smiled with me anymore. I loved that woman badly. I didn't breathe the same without her.

Thank God she wasn't alone and she didn't cry all the time anymore. In the footage, she was eating pizza and drinking Patron like she didn't have a husband that missed the fuck out of her.

I continued to watch the video, wishing I was the one sitting at home with my fine Azuri. I wouldn't have even minded if her friend was also there with us. I'd fuck them both.

My naughty thoughts were halted when I saw that this female had started kissing in my wife. I cried real tears. My wife kissed her back with so much passion. Damn, I was just daydreaming of fucking them both but it's different when the bitch was actually in my home fucking on my wife without me there to participate. At that moment, I vowed to kill that woman, even if it was the last thing I did before I died.

I watched her bending before Zuri and spreading her legs wide. Damn, I could tell my wife's panties were soaked. The woman licked and nibbled on Azuri's pretty pink pussy while Zuri closed her eyes.

Before I knew it, Azuri had removed a fucking gun from beneath the couch and popped the bitch.

I replayed the video and watched it a million times in
disbelief.

What the fuck had been happening? As far as I knew Azuri wouldn't harm a fly!

Where the hell did Azuri get a gun? There were so many unanswered questions.

I was confused. Everything was falling apart. What had my wife gotten herself into? How was I suppose to protect her now?

I continued watching the video while Azuri fucked our house up. Did she set up her friend?

Was Zuri some sort of traitor? She then made a call and reported a murder to…*Chyn?*

What were the chances that my wife was hanging with the same bitch that I was fucking?

At this point, my eyes were glued to the phone screen. I started sweating. I was wet with sweat all over and the air conditioner was on.

My wife then opened the door and eleven other bitches entered my house with guns pointing towards her. They seem to be searching my house. Two of the women bent and examined the dead woman. They all seemed to be crying. More surprisingly, Azuri started crying hysterically again as she gave her account of what happened.

The door buzzed again and in walked Chyn…

My fucking eyes bulged.

I threw the phone down and grabbed my gun. Something was definitely going on and until I knew what it was, I wasn't safe and neither was my wife.

I was about to run outside the house to my car, but the door opened at the same time.

"Going somewhere?" Chyn asked.

"I was about to get some weed," I replied quickly.

"I've got enough for both of us. Come roll up with me, babe," she said as she kissed my lips.

I kissed her back, involuntarily. I didn't want to kiss this bitch. But somehow my body, heart, and brain never agreed when it came to this pretty devil. I was falling for her. I couldn't allow myself to love her, not right now. If something happened to Zuri, I'd never be able to forgive myself.

I kissed her with as much passion as I could muster, considering the revelation I'd just experienced. I felt afraid. I felt like a coward. She had bigger balls than I did. I didn't half fuck her though, I fucked the shit out of her. I was turned on. She'd started to grow on me. I thought about her. I thought about Azuri. It's like they had both started to merge into the same person.

If I was going to settle for a bad bitch, why not take the baddest of them all? Chyn had Zuri beat in that arena.

The video footage that I saw made me view wifey in a different light. I didn't mean to assume the worse. I'd listened to Zuri talking and laughing with this lady. Spilling her guts to this lady and crying on her shoulders numerous times. At the end of the day regardless of what Kat did, I'd prefer Zuri to be straight up about what the beef was.

The lady thought they were friends and Zuri snuck a shot.

I just couldn't be optimistic about this. A snake was a snake.

I'd ensure that Azuri was okay and that no harm was ever going to come her way. I genuinely love this girl but I'd walk away from her though. She deceived me into thinking she was sweet and innocent. I could never trust her the same.

With Chyn, what you saw was what you got. She wouldn't kill her friend while her eyes were closed. If she drew her gun, you'd have a fair chance to pull yours too.

Only cowards stabbed people in their backs.

* * *

I thought it over for days. I literally became sick with thoughts of my wife being such a whack bitch. The days that I spent moving around and thinking the worst of Azuri provided me with clarity. The boy I was fifteen years ago loved Azuri to death and was loyal.

But the man that I've become craves Chyn. Every day, I had to convince myself that I was still in live. The truth is, I didn't love Azuri anymore.

I've evolved. Chyn fits the man that I am today to the tee. She has crept in and stolen the only real asset I had: my heart.

So…. I've decidedly become 'Team Chyn'.

I'm giving Azuri the divorce she so badly wants and sending her home to Vel. She was no longer the woman that I needed. She was a backstabbing snake, and with the type of business I'm in, I just cannot take the risk.

My heart ached but with Azuri gone, I could pursue endless possibilities.

See, there are many things that I could've achieved but they all took risks and with Azuri around, I never wanted my secret street life to ever affect her. Chyn didn't give a fuck and seems to already be knee-deep in the street shit so she'd understand the risks. Plus, she could protect herself.

With a bitch like her on my dick, I could become the king of the streets.

Chyn has about to be 'dick-whipped' into becoming the Bonnie to my Clyde.

Chapter 16:
Chyn

Like every other time in my life, I'd work my butt off to achieve something and when I got it, I no longer wanted it.

Kloud was becoming annoying. He was around me and beneath me all the time. He no longer seemed to be infatuated with his wife. He hasn't even been sneaking out or anything these days. He was legit trying to get in my good graces.

At first, I was thrilled that I seemed to be winning but then something triggered inside me. If he wasn't loyal to someone he was in a relationship with for over a decade, why would he stay loyal to me? I was no better than her. She was just as pretty and she was accomplished. Plus, she genuinely loved him. A lot more than I did.

I reflected on my life and my goals. Apart

from blazing guns and selling drugs, I wanted to settle down and start a family. I didn't know how "Mommy Chyn" and "queen-pin Chyn" would co-exist but I was willing to try.

Kloud had all the qualities that I wanted in my future husband. I admit, he had a few glitches but I'm sure we could work on ironing them out.

It was time to reveal to Kloud that I knew he was married. Just to see where his head was.

Somehow, I always had to be spiteful and sinister. I hadn't been fucking with Azuri at all since Kat's death. I didn't include her in any of our plans or anything. I straight-up ignored her like the plague. I still felt like she knew more bout Kat's death than she told us and I would find out if it's the last thing I did before I died.

I called all my friends from the Moneybag clan and invited them to dinner. As an afterthought, I also invited Azuri. I told them all that they could bring dates because I wanted to introduce them to someone special.

I had decided to end the cat and mouse thing with Kloud and Azuri once and for all. He would learn how savage I could truly be. If there's any chance of us ever having a future together, he needed to know that I ran the streets and even *he* answered to me, albeit indirectly. The only person I, in turn, answered to was Velasquez.

Answering to him wasn't even a big deal. He trusted me with his life. I called all shots from all angles basically.

I had made a tattoo appointment to get the word "queen" tatted on my left shoulder blade with the crown on top of the letter Q. It was symbolic because I *am* the Queen.

After finishing up my tattoo appointment, I went shopping for the special date that I had planned. I got myself a maroon and gold two-piece skirt suit. I ensured that my shoulders and cleavage would be on display. I copped Kloud a maroon Giuseppe long-sleeved shirt with gold trimmings and, as luck would have it, the word King was stitched around the top in big gold print.

I called and made a reservation at my favourite restaurant, 'Top Notch'. I rented out the entire top deck and asked that they decorate it for a short-notice dinner party. The theme was "Crown Her".

I ran all my errands for the day before calling Kloud and inviting him to the dinner party. I told him I was celebrating the life of my dead friend. He bit the hook and agreed to attend the dinner. I then told him that I'd already bought him a shirt and made recommendations for the pants and shoes he could complement it with.

I got home in time to get ready for the dinner party. When I got home, Kloud had already started getting dressed. He looked yummy with his new Mohawk haircut and I just couldn't help myself. I entered the bathroom and stood behind him. He stood in front of the mirror popping in his diamond earrings. I studied him carefully looking for a single flaw. He was absolutely perfect.

I slid my arms around his waist from behind and prompted him to face me.

I started to kiss him with all the passion that I could muster. He kissed me fervently.

The dinner party could wait.

I had to fuck him right now because if things didn't go how I hoped they would tonight, I'd be killing somebody.

As we kissed, I dropped my robe, revealing my nakedness beneath. His eyes roved over my entire body and I saw a little twinkle in his eyes. He bent before me and prompted me to bent my knees so that he could position my feet around his shoulders and my pussy in his face.

I was gone as he lifted me effortlessly.

He stiffened his tongue and started to tongue fuck me in mid-air like I weighed no more than a bag of chips.

I screamed and quivered and begged him to stop, while he licked my pussy relentlessly.

After about the fourth orgasm and me feeling like I died a thousand deaths, he finally let me down. He stood me on my feet and I almost fell. He laughed and motioned for me to turn around. I did.

As I turned around, he lifted my arms from my sides and positioned them above my head. He proceeded to tie my hands with one of the towels from the rack.

After ensuring that my hands were secured, he pushed head downwards and tapped my back motioning for me to toot my ass up. I assumed the position.

He started massaging my already tender clitoris and my body responded. I started to moan out his name. He moved his finger from my clit and replaced it with his cock. He thrust into me aggressively and plummeted me non-stop. I liked it rough. I met him mid-thrust each time until he gave up the quest of trying to bring me towards the elusive orgasm.

He stood still and I gyrated on his penis. I whined and shook my hips, rolling them back and forth. I was enjoying myself and he was shouting inaudible sweet nothings in my ears.

I half turned so that I could look at him while I was flinging it back on his dick. He lost control and started a fast, rhythmic stroke. He was going to climax soon.

"Babe, cum with me," he demanded, and my body responded.

He ejaculated deep inside me and I fell to a puddle on the floor as he removed his penis from my vagina. He stood above me and I looked up at his flaccid penis. I didn't know how I was going to function without this penis in my life if things went awry tonight.

"Untie my hands," I requested. "We need to start getting ready."

I turned on the bathroom sound system and took a shower. I was living in paradise at the moment. I hoped it lasted. I prayed that it would last.

God, answer me this one prayer because if he messes up in front of my girls, I'm bodying him and I'm bodying Azuri.

He'd better pick the right bitch tonight.

Chapter 17:
Kloud
Moment of Truth

I've been rocking with Chyn for a minute, but we've never really gone to anywhere up-scale …or anything.

So, I was happy to be going on a real date with her. She invited me in the spur of the moment to have dinner with her and her friends so we could celebrate the life of her late friend, Katura.

Thinking of it now, I feel like a little bitch. I mean, I know that I have my own life that I'm trying to keep hidden from Chyn. That's why I was yet to introduce her to any of my friends or anything.

But what was *she* hiding?

I felt a twinge of guilt because I knew that my

wife had been the one to kill Katura. So now, attending a party in her honour, felt like some snake-shit.

I still haven't had the time to find out from Azuri what exactly was going on. I'm no a snitch. I'm staying out of this war as much as possible. I didn't even know how Azuri became associated with the likes of Chyn and Kat.

When we arrived at the restaurant, Chyn made a phone call and we were directed to an underground parking lot with exactly eleven other cars. I was amazed because I'd been to this restaurant before and I hadn't even know that they had private parking.

I could get used to this life.

Chyn stepped out of the car from the passenger side and gave herself a quick once over. She took a tiny mirror from her purse and stared at her reflection. Minutes passed before she decided to reapply her lip gloss.

She looked absolutely flawless.

She has gotten a new tattoo of the word "Queen". It accentuated her shoulder and she wore her hair up in a cute up-do with an 'all natural' make-up look.

She had chosen maroon and gold clothing for both of us and boy, did she look like royalty. She wore a tank top and skirt set. The skirt had deep splits in the front center *and* back center. She looked super sexy tonight. I'd forego the entire dinner and go back home just to fuck her to death.

She walked by my side looking all cute and innocent.

We were also both in deep thought, it seemed. I wondered what she was thinking about while standing by my side.

We entered the elevator and I asked her to choose what floor as I really had no idea where she was taking me. Instead of answering, she pressed the R button and the elevator started to move.

She then asked me, "Are you nervous?"

I kissed her hungrily and replied, "I'm not

nervous to meet your friends because at the end of the day, fuck what they think. What I'm nervous about is that my dick refuses to stay down."

She laughed.

Ding! The elevator stopped and she stepped out. She was greeted by a plethora of ladies. They all hugged her and kissed her cheeks.

It was obvious her friends loved her dearly.

She then cleared her throat and introduced me, "Everyone, this is Kloud. He's my friend… A very *good* friend."

They all *ooohed* and *ahhhed* and sized me up. One that was identified as Jazzy finally broke the ice.

"So this is why Chyn has been so calm lately," she said. "The boss lady has been getting the D on the regular. *Okurrrrr.*" She squealed and stuck her tongue out while twerking.

They all hugged me as if they'd known me for years. The last girl that hugged me, I knew her very well. Her name was Angel. She was my supplier. I had even gone to see her earlier. Turns, out she didn't want to supply me anymore and wasn't interested in an increase in her price.

Nothing. She'd just straight up told me that "effective today", she wouldn't be supplying me with any more product until further notice.

I'd wanted to wring her delicate looking neck. We didn't have any beef, no disagreements or bad blood. She'd just made the decision as a spur of the moment thing, I guess. I was ordered to close the shop also and stop distributing on her turf. No explanations. Nothing. It seemed suspect because we'd always had a very good business relationship.

But she hugged me also while staring deep into my eyes. It was almost as if she was challenging me. She acted like she didn't even know me so I followed her lead.

So, I hugged her back and introduced myself.

Everyone laughed and we all got seated; a total of twelve men and twelve women. I also noticed that there were two empty seats but didn't comment.

We chit-chatted about numerous topics and laughed over drinks. Music was playing in the background too, and I was having fun. I'd not had any real fun in years. I'd even started to drink, and laughed and made jokes as if I'd known these people forever.

Chyn's cell phone then rang and she walked off to answer it.

I didn't know who called but somehow we all felt a shift in her mood. When she returned to the table, she wouldn't stop checking her watch every two seconds, and I myself started to get nervous.

To break the ice, I asked Chyn to dance with me. At first, she was reluctant but then she changed her mind. When she finally started twerking on me and giggling like a schoolgirl, the doors opened and in walked my wife.

She didn't see me immediately. She looked around and if looks could kill, honestly I'd be dead. Our eyes connected and I turned my head away.

I pushed Chyn away and started to walk towards Azuri as she turned around to exit the dinner party. Chyn was directly behind me.

"Where the fuck are you going?" she questioned, loudly.

By this time everyone's attention was drawn to the drama that was unfolding. I ignored her and ran off. I was trying to catch up with my wife. She deserved an explanation even if we were separated.

Chyn yelled after me but I continued. I never wanted to hurt Zuri. I felt fucked. I wanted to love and protect Azuri forever but I'd fallen in love with someone else.

I stopped.

Azuri stepped outside but then came back inside immediately. It was like she had changed her mind about the confrontation.

At this point, I was one step from standing directly in front of Zuri and I could hear Chyn's heels clicking across the tiles as she approached us hurriedly.

I didn't know what to do or say. My instincts somehow started to warn me that this dinner party was a set up.

"Azuri, how do you know Chyn?" I questioned, calmly even though I was heated. I was going to fuck Azuri all the way up too if she didn't think clearly before she answered.

Chyn walked quickly because she had stepped in the middle of Azuri and I.

She interjected, "Azuri, do you want to tell me what the fuck is happening here?"

"Wait… What do you mean? You're the one fucking my husband and you wanna question *me*?" she hissed.

"Boss or no boss, *fuck* you, Chyn, and you're little Barbie cronies. By the way, that's my no-good husband that I'm divorcing, but I'm sure you already knew that."

Smack.

Chyn slapped Azuri in the face. She lost her balance and fell to the ground. Azuri tried to recover and regain her footing but Chyn seemed to be in her zone. She started to kick Zuri violently and stomp on her. She was as strong as a lion.

As quickly as the shock wore off, I tried to lift Chyn away from Zuri's bloodied body.

None of Chyn's friends tried to stop the fight. Instead, they were all on go, because as soon as I was able to pull the women apart, I turned to ask for help to stop the fight but was halted in my tracks.

"Put her down," Angel pointed her gun towards me and took it off safety.

I laughed.
"You're not serious," I said, incredulously.

I heard a click, then, "You heard her. Put Chyn down!"

Three more guns were pointed at me.

I put her down.

Chyn stood before me. "When were you planning to tell me that you were married?"

I walked away. I heard clicks and continued walking.

Chyn called out to me but I continued walking. I loved Chyn but I'd promised to protect Azuri. I scooped my wife's beaten body from the ground and made my way to the exit.

At the end of the day, I'm a man. I had my pride and Chyn crossed the line tonight. Boss or no boss, *I* aligned the dick and if she didn't understand that, the relationship couldn't continue past tonight.

Pow!

A shot rang out. I was about to turn to face Chyn and ask that she cut the bullshit.

Pow, pow, pow! Three more shots rang out.

I felt blood soaking through my shirt. Azuri was shot. I laid her body on the floor. She was dead.

My wife was dead and I blamed myself. I kissed her cheek and closed her eyes.

"That's for Kat, bitch," Jazzie shouted.

And I realized that the vendetta against Azuri wasn't about me. It was because she killed their friend.

I stood and faced Chyn after closing Azuri's eyes.

"Give me a good reason to not kill you too," she said, way too calmly. I instantly felt chilled.

"Chyn, believe me. I never meant to hurt you. I should've told you that I'm married but I didn't. Was that really a valid reason for killing my wife? This doesn't in anyway builds your boss image. Bosses don't kill women over their husbands. Bosses find their own husbands."

She sighed. "Don't get it twisted, honey. I run shit around here. Oh, and your wife is dead because she killed Kat. Not because we shared a dick."

I stood still.

"What?" she continued. "You didn't think I'd find out? I have your phones and car tapped. Absolutely nothing moves in this city without my permission."

She whispered something to Angel, who then walked away with her phone held to her ear.

My head pounded. I was confused. My wife was dead and I was unknowingly fucking around with the biggest drug and gun distributor in Jamaica.

How did I miss the signs?

I thought quickly. "I know I lied about some stuff. From my heart, I never meant to hurt you. At one point I was no longer concerned with Azuri. We were getting a divorce so it was no longer necessary to bring up my marriage." I spoke truthfully. "Just give me some time to bury Azuri and set up our affairs and I'll be right back to you."

I pleaded with her.

"Put your guns down," she announced then turned back to me. "I don't know what kind of affairs you're going to get in order because your warehouse was just burnt flat. So now you have no income. No money and no wife."

The men started to scramble toward the exit. Nobody wanted to be associated with these crazy bitches.

I was stuck though. If I made the wrong

choice, I'd be laying right next to my dead wife. If I chose Chyn, I'd be betraying my wife's memory. But if I tried walking away from Chyn. I'd be as dead as Azuri.

Cheating always hurt all the parties involved. It rarely ended well.

My heart beat wildly in my chest and I sweated profusely. The right choice was to tell Chyn to go fuck herself. But what would I gain from that? I might end up on the floor beside my wife.

Or I could forget Azuri. She was already dead. And I could move on with Chyn.

I was undecided.

So what was it going to be?

Chyn or Azuri?

Thanks for reading!

Stay tuned for

"*Memoirs of a Bad Bitch 2*"

Made in the USA
Columbia, SC
07 July 2020

12322803R00090